W9-CKM-654

The Dwarf Dinosaur

The Dwarf Dinosaur

Esther A. Barnes

VANTAGE PRESS
New York

Illustrated by Jeffrey V. Mayes

FIRST EDITION

Published by Vantage Press, Inc.
516 West 34th Street, New York, New York 10001

Manufactured in the United States of America
ISBN: 0-533-11103-X

0 9 8 7 6 5 4 3 2 1

To my grandson Norman, for his love of dinosaurs

This book was also inspired by my other grandchildren: Tom (Tuma) and Kimberly (Kuma).

The Dwarf Dinosaur

Millions of years ago, in a land far away, lived Mr. and Mrs. Dinosaur. They didn't have any children, but they wanted a child very much.

While they were waiting and hoping for a child, they passed the time eating the vegetation of the land. They were very peaceful dinosaurs.

Finally, one day when Mr. and Mrs. Dinosaur had gone for a walk, Mrs. Dinosaur went off by herself. After a while, Mr. Dinosaur found her again only to discover that she had laid a very small egg.

Now the brontosauruses are very large animals, so you can imagine the look on Mr. Dinosaur's face when he saw such a small egg.

"Oh, no matter," said Mr. Dinosaur to Mrs. Dinosaur. "I am sure he will grow up just fine; after all, he is our little son." (Mr. Dinosaur said *he* because he had always wanted a son.)

When the baby was hatched, he was very, very small, but they loved him anyway. You see, he was their son, and Mommy and Daddy dinosaurs always love their little dinosaurs.

Mommy and Daddy named their son Norman, because he was a very noble and courageous fellow.

Though months and years went by, Norman never got very large because he was a dwarf dinosaur. He had a lot of problems to overcome and a lot of things to learn. But in spite of his size, he was a very brave and smart dinosaur.

One day Norman was out playing with some of his friends when a very large meat-eating dinosaur came along. All of Norman's friends ran away. Because Norman was so small, he didn't see the meat-eating dinosaur coming until it was right on top of him; and because he was so small, he was able to hide between two rocks, out of reach. Norman was very glad then that he was a little dinosaur.

Another time, Norman was playing near a tree when a large snakelike creature came down from the tree and almost got him. Again, Norman got away through a narrow path. He could run very fast.

Still another time, Norman was being chased by a large meat-eating dinosaur, and in his hurry to get away, he fell off a cliff. Luckily for him there was a large lake below.

KERPLUNK! Down he went into the water!

That is how Norman learned to swim. Boy, did he like swimming! He swam around and around. Norman had a grand time!

But now Norman was far from home, and he couldn't find his way back after falling off the cliff. He wasn't sure which way to go, so he just kept wandering, getting farther and farther away from home.

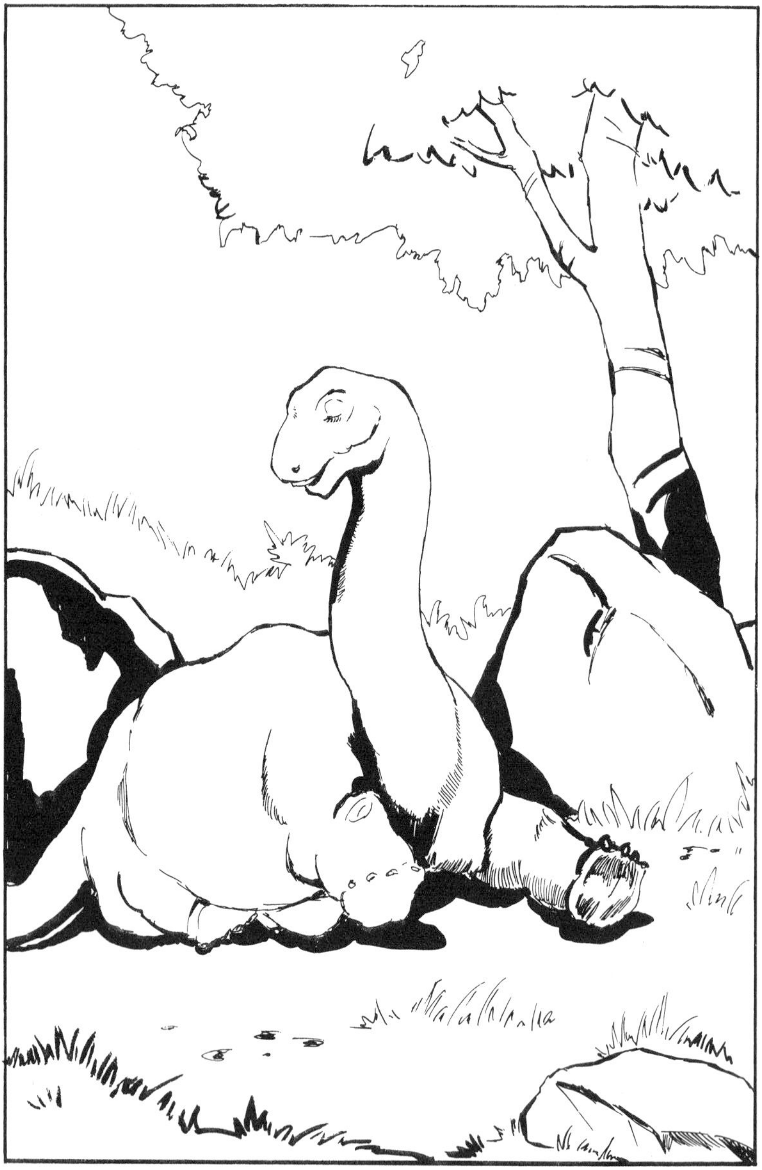

Finally, he came upon a beautiful meadow full of grass and flowers. It was so nice, he rested after he ate his meal.

After a few days, though, Norman decided to move on. He was still very lonely and could not find his family.

Norman finally decided he would look for a dinosaur just like himself. As he went farther on his way, Norman met many small animals, but he didn't find any friendly dinosaurs. He was so very lonely.

By now, he was an adult dinosaur, but Norman still wasn't over two feet tall. Oh, how he wished to find a little lady dinosaur like himself so he wouldn't be so lonely!

As the little dinosaur ventured forth, he encountered many species of animals, but he could find nothing like himself.

One day Norman heard a flapping of wings. He looked up just in time because he was being chased by a winged reptile that had decided to eat him for lunch! Norman ran and ran as fast as his little legs could carry him, until he came to a small opening in a cave. The winged reptile could not get through.

In the little dinosaur's haste, he slipped on some slippery rocks and went zooming down a crevice and went **KERPLUNK** into an underground river. After a while, he was able to swim to shore, but he didn't know where he was or how to get to the outside world again.

Norman wandered aimlessly to and fro, up and down, because there was such little light in the cave. He went farther and came to a glowing section of the cave, which was caused by a

phosphorus rock (a rock that shines in the dark). He could see his surroundings very clearly now. He started to relax a little and tried to figure out where he was. Norman finally decided which way he would go.

He went downhill farther and farther when **FINALLY,** at the end of the path, he saw a glimmer of light. He went about a thousand more feet. Lo and behold, he found a hole to the outside that even *he* couldn't fit through!

Norman wandered and wandered, trying to find a way out. He was so tired of eating mushrooms, which was the only thing he could find to eat in the cave. Norman longed for nice sweet grass.

All of a sudden, out of the blue, the cave began to rumble, shake, and quiver as a volcano erupted at the top of the mountain.

The little dinosaur got trapped in a tiny hollow pocket of air and had to stay there for several weeks. He was trapped, but he was safe from the terrible volcano outside!

Luckily Norman could still breathe and there were mushrooms in the air pocket, but it was very dark and he had to feel his way around. He was very frightened and confused. He couldn't understand what was happening to the world around him.

Finally, Norman was able to push through the rubble around him and escape. About five hundred yards farther down the cave, he found an opening that he could get through, but the ground was very hot from the volcano so he had to wait until it cooled down. He waited patiently for the ground to cool, so that he could walk on it. Then, Norman ventured forth and continued on his journey, still looking for someone so he wouldn't be so frightened and lonely.

Norman found small mounds of grass that the lava from the volcano had not gotten to. Norman was so small that he didn't need much to eat anyway.

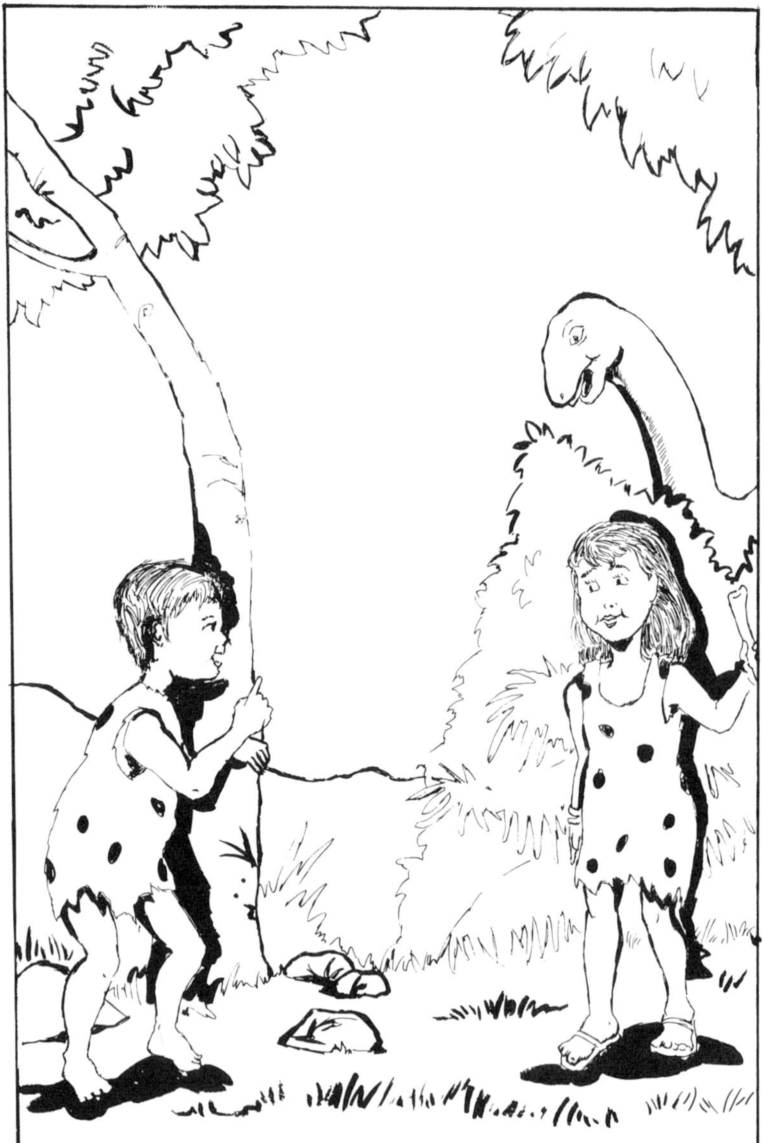

He was very happy to be alive. He found he loved life even if he was alone. He thought he would be alone the rest of his life.

One day, Norman saw something move. He followed the object at a safe distance because he didn't know what it was. Norman discovered two of the strangest-looking creatures he had ever seen. You see, they were a boy and girl who lived in a cave. They didn't know what to think of the little dwarf dinosaur either.

For several weeks, they played hide-and-seek with each other. Each day, they

each grew braver and braver and got closer and closer to each other. They were all so curious!

Finally, they just stood and looked at each other, and this time they did not run away.

The boy and girl cave people offered Norman grass, and he ate it right from their hands! They all became friends and had many adventures together.

Tuma was the name of the little boy, and Kuma was the name of the little girl. Norman, Tuma, and Kuma were all very happy together. They were friends forever.